D1179069

Hare
and Guy Fawkes

The Little Grey Rabbit Library

Hare and
Guy Fawkes

Alison Uttley
pictures by Margaret Tempest

Collins

William Collins Sons & Co Ltd
London · Glasgow · Sydney · Auckland
Toronto · Johannesburg

First published 1956
© text The Alison Uttley Literary Property Trust 1986
© illustrations The Estate of Margaret Tempest 1986
This arrangement © William Collins Sons & Co Ltd 1986
Cover decoration by Fiona Owen
Decorated capital by Mary Cooper
Alison Uttley's original story has been abridged for this book.
Uttley, Alison
Hare and Guy Fawkes. — Rev.ed —
(Little Grey Rabbit books)
I. Title II Tempest, Margaret
III. Series
823'912 [J] PZ7

ISBN 0-00-194216-6

Made and Printed in Great Britain by
William Collins Sons and Co Ltd, Glasgow

FOREWORD

Of course you must understand that Grey Rabbit's home had no electric light or gas, and even the candles were made from pith of rushes dipped in wax from the wild bees' nests, which Squirrel found. Water there was in plenty, but it did not come from a tap. It flowed from a spring outside, which rose up from the ground and went to a brook. Grey Rabbit cooked on a fire, but it was a wood fire, there was no coal in that part of the country. Tea did not come from India, but from a little herb known very well to country people, who once dried it and used it in their cottage homes. Bread was baked from wheat ears, ground fine, and Hare and Grey Rabbit gleaned in the cornfields to get the wheat.

The doormats were plaited rushes, like country-made mats, and cushions were stuffed with wool gathered from the hedges where sheep pushed through the thorns. As for the looking-glass, Grey Rabbit found the glass, dropped from a lady's handbag, and Mole made a frame for it. Usually the animals gazed at themselves in the still pools as so many country children have done. The country ways of Grey Rabbit were the country ways known to the author.

t was November and the north wind blew fiercely. It caught hold of the trees and shook them till the leaves fell down in showers.

Hare was very busy. He had a besom of birch twigs and he swept up the leaves which lay like a carpet. Brown, crimson, gold and amber leaves were there, and he flicked them away to a heap.

"Lots of letters with no writing on them," he called to Squirrel.

Squirrel stooped and picked up a handful and examined them carefully.

"There *is* writing, Hare," she cried. "It says, 'wind' on one and 'ice' on another and 'snow' on another."

"Whatever it says, I'm going to have a bonfire," said Hare.

"Why?" asked Squirrel. "We have a good fire in the kitchen."

Hare suddenly leapt astride the besom and rode it as if it were a horse.

"Gee-up! Gee-up!" he chirped, "I'm making a bonfire for a secret."

"Silly old Hare," laughed Squirrel. "We all know you can't keep a secret."

"Then I'll tell you," said Hare, and he got off his twiggy horse and whispered in Squirrel's ear.

"Soft! Soft! It's bonfire night very soon. I heard from Robin the postman who heard from the village children."

"What is that?" asked Squirrel.

"I don't know, but I am sweeping the leaves to make the bonfire like everyone else in the great wide world."

Grey Rabbit came up the path from the field where she had been gathering firewood. She was surprised to see Hare so busy.

"Thank you, dear Hare," said she. "Thank you for tidying the garden."

"I'm not tidying the garden," cried Hare, indignantly. "It's a bonfire for Guy Fawkes, same as Robin told me."

"What is that?" asked Grey Rabbit.

"I'm sure I don't know," replied Hare, and he went on with his sweeping.

"I'll ask Milkman Hedgehog tomorrow," said Grey Rabbit.

That night Wise Owl flew over hooting a
new-old song.

> "Too-whit! Too-whoo!
> Whatever you do,
> Remember, remember,
> The Fifth of November,
> Too-whit! Too-whoo!
> Remember."

When Old Hedgehog brought the milk the
next morning, Grey Rabbit asked him about
bonfire night.

Hedgehog lifted his wooden pail of new frothy milk and filled the little jug.

"I'll tell 'ee," said Hedgehog, solemnly. "It's an old ancient custom. Fireworks! Bonfire! Toffee! Parkin! It's a dangerous night down in the village with bangs and flashes of fire and lights in the sky. I keeps indoors, safe. Wise Owl was warning you to keep indoors, Mister Hare, and not to get into no mischief."

Of course this excited Hare, and he simply had to go off to the village.

"Take care," warned Grey Rabbit.

"I want to ask my friend the Pussy Cat about this custom," said Hare. "She will know because she lives at the village shop and hears the news."

He galloped away over the fields and into the village. He crept softly in the shadows of the cottages and his heart beat with excitement as he sidled to the village shop window.

He expected the little shop to have its plates of home-made cakes and lollypops, its muffins and crusty loaves, but when he looked in he saw a tray piled with very pretty things. They were long and short, fat and thin, dumpy and tiny, striped and starred, in blue, scarlet and gold.

Hare licked his lips. "Goodies!" said he. "Candies! Sugar-candy and barley-sticks, like rainbows."

The cat sat washing herself on the doorstep. She nodded at Hare.

"Miaow! Good evening, Mister Hare. Come to admire our fireworks?" she asked.

14

"Fireworks? I thought they were goodies," said Hare in surprise.

"No. Can't eat 'em. They are to let off on bonfire night, to frighten Guy Fawkes," said the Cat.

"Could I – could we – could you —?" stammered Hare. "I've got no money."

"I'll give you a few," said the Cat, casually. "My mistress owes me something for catching the mice. Just go round the corner."

Hare vanished behind a bush and the Cat calmly entered the shop, leapt in the window and grabbed some crackers in her paws.

"Puss! What are you doing?" called Mrs Bunting.

"Mee-iaow!" mewed the Cat and she dashed out to Hare.

"Quick! Take these! Light one at a time. Be careful! Catherine wheels, rockets, and jumping-jacks and a fountain!" she hissed.

"Puss! What have you done with those fireworks?" called Mrs Bunting anxiously, but the Cat returned to the doorstep and went on washing her face.

Mrs Bunting peered around, sighing, "Oh you naughty Puss!"

Hare was already galloping down the lane with his prizes and when he was safely away from the village he stopped and looked at the crackers. He gently licked one, but the smell of gunpowder made him wrinkle his nose.

"Not a very nice smell," he thought.

Grey Rabbit and Squirrel were glad to see him, and they held up the pretty toys he had brought. Hare boldly put a small cracker in the fire, to find what would happen.

It flew out with a loud bang and then chased Hare round the room, leaping after him as if it were alive. Hare leapt too. He darted away and jumped on the table, while little Grey Rabbit and Squirrel laughed till tears came to their eyes.

"That was a live jumping-jack," said Hare.

"Are you all right?" called a voice at the door, and Moldy Warp came in.

"That was a jumping-jack," boasted Hare. "It made us jump like anything. I jumped the highest because I'm a Hare."

"Yes, you did," agreed Squirrel.

"I'm rather like a jumping-jack myself, don't you think so?" continued Hare.

He sprang about the room, jerking to one side and the other in big leaps, calling "Bang! Bang! Bang!"

Moldy Warp picked up the fireworks and looked at each.

"These are what the children let off in the village," said he. "I've seen them but I keep away."

Grey Rabbit picked them up with the shovel and carried them outside.

"There! No more fireworks for us, thank you Hare," said she.

"You can make a bonfire and have parkin and bonfire toffee with treacle in it," said Moldy Warp.

"I've collected the leaves ready for the bonfire," said Hare, eagerly, "and I can make the bonfire toffee, and taste a bit."

"Squirrel and I will make the parkin," added Grey Rabbit. "There's some oatmeal left from the oats we gathered in the cornfield, and treacle in the jug and honeycomb and butter."

So they started to make the good things and while they cooked, Moldy Warp told them about Guy Fawkes Day.

"There's a queer fellow called the Guy," he began mysteriously. "He is made of rags and sticks. The children pop him on the bonfire top, and they let off fireworks and they all sing 'Remember, remember, the Fifth of November'."

Hare pondered all this, and when Moldy Warp went home and the brown sticky toffee was made, he wandered in the garden. He picked up the fireworks and put them in a dry place. "How would it be if we asked the Fox to be the Guy?" he suggested to Squirrel.

"Really, Hare, you are foolish," retorted Squirrel. "The Fox wouldn't and you might be eaten up."

"Perhaps it is rather dangerous," said Hare, dreamily.

On Guy Fawkes Day Hare started off across the fields to invite the Speckledy Hen to the bonfire. On the way he saw the Fox slouching in the same direction.

"Hallo, Hare," cried the Fox cheerfully. "Where are you going so fast?"

"To see the Speckledy Hen," stammered Hare.

"So am I! Isn't that a coincidence!" said the Fox.

"Yes, it is," said Hare.

"What?" asked the Fox.

"What you said. A co-co-incidence," said poor Hare.

"This is a special day," said the Fox.

"It's Guy Fawkes Day, and we're having a bonfire," said Hare.

"And who's the Guy?" asked the Fox.

Hare became bolder. "Will you be the Guy, Mr Fox?" he asked.

"Delighted, my dear Hare," smiled the Fox.

"Then come to our party tonight," invited Hare.

"We might play noughts and crosses," laughed the Fox. He was in such a good humour he decided not to bother about Speckledy Hen, and waving his paw, he turned aside.

"Speckledy Hen! Will you come to our bonfire tonight?" panted Hare, as he darted into the farmyard.

"Who was that fine gentleman?" asked the Speckledy Hen, sternly. "Who was that creature in a brown coat? Do you keep bad company, Hare?"

"It was the Fox," confessed Hare. "He's coming too."

Speckledy Hen was so flustered she beat her wings against Hare to send him away.

"Are you mad, Hare?" she cried.

"Sorry, Speckledy Hen," panted Hare. "But he's going to be the Guy."

"The Guy? Well, I *will* come to the bonfire party but I shall stand in the doorway and watch," said the Hen.

Hare went home with his head buzzing with secrets and fears and alarms. He told Grey Rabbit and Squirrel of his plans.

Grey Rabbit turned pale and Squirrel ran to the top of the bonfire and there she sat.

"Come down," shouted Hare. "You will be burned when we set it alight. That's for the Guy."

"The Fox isn't as foolish as you," muttered Squirrel, but she came down and went to tie a ribbon on her tail.

As soon as the first star appeared in the sky, and the first shadow of dusk came among the trees, Moldy Warp with Fuzzypeg and Old Hedgehog and the Speckledy Hen came tripping through the gate and up the garden path. Speckledy Hen brought three potatoes to be baked in the bonfire. Fuzzypeg had his book of Fables under his arm.

"I shall read a tale to the Fox if he is unkind to Grey Rabbit," said he.

Hare pinned a Catherine wheel to the trunk of an apple tree. He struck a match and set it alight. The flaming wheel spun round and round with blue and lavender rings of light and a shower of golden sparks.

"Oh-o-o-o-o," they all cried.

"It's like a spinning rainbow," said Grey Rabbit.

"It's magical," thought the Fox, who was watching over the wall. "I daren't go near that burning wheel."

Then Hare put a dumpy little firework on the earth and Squirrel set it alight. She sprang away and a shower of golden rain fell from a fiery fountain.

"That's a Roman candle," said Hare.

"Roman magic," murmured the astonished Fox over the wall.

Hare opened a small box and gave a large match to each animal, except of course the Hen in the doorway.

"These are Bengal lights," said he, "you must wave them round your heads."

So Fuzzypeg and Moldy Warp, Mr Hedgehog, Squirrel, and Grey Rabbit obeyed Hare, and as he lighted their matches they swung them in circles over their heads. Rings of blue and green and red light appeared, and everyone enjoyed them except the Fox.

Finally Hare put a rocket with its long stick in the ground. He lighted the fuse and rushed away with warning cries.

"Look out," he called.

"Ss-ss-ss-ss-ss," hissed the rocket and it flew so high in the air they all thought it would hit the stars. It seemed to go for ever, and they stared upward crying, "Oo-oo-oo-oo."

Down came the little blue balloons of fire which disappeared in streaks of gold.

"Hare is a magician," whispered the Fox.

Hare lighted the bonfire, and a flame soared upward. All the leaves shone like gold as they fluttered up into the evening sky. "Wind, ice, snow," sang the leaves in thin piping voices, and the stars looked down to see what kind of bonfire this was with little animals dancing round it.

"Please, Mister Hare, may I come in? I'm the Guy," said a quaking voice, and the Fox looked through the gate.

"Yes, come in Guy Fawkes," said Hare, bravely. "Would you like to sit on the bonfire?"

"No thank you," said the Fox, "but if you will give me a firework I shall be happy."

"Here's the last. It's a jumping-jack," said Hare.

The Fox took the jumping-jack and slowly lighted it with a glowing twig from the fire. Then he held it up.

Bang! Bang! Bang! it went, darting after him, hitting him on the nose, singeing his tail, burning his toes. It jumped wherever the Fox jumped, so he leapt over the wall. After him the little jumping-jack went, and it followed him into the wood, until finally it fizzled out with a hiss of laughter.

How they all laughed to see the Fox run! Grey Rabbit fetched a plate of parkin cut into small pieces, and Squirrel held out the tin of bonfire toffee. They ate the good things by the light of the burning fire, and again they danced round it.

At last the fire burned low, and Hare raked from the embers the three hot baked potatoes. They divided them for supper.

It was bedtime, and they said good night to the bonfire, and went into the little house and shut the door. The Speckledy Hen slept in the kitchen and little Fuzzypeg was wrapped up in a rug on the floor. Mr Hedgehog and Moldy Warp walked home without him, singing as they went.

But the next morning Fuzzypeg ran out to look at the ring of ashes left by the bonfire. He stirred the burnt leaves and among them he found something. It was like a little star, sparkling and glittering with light.

"We hit something out of the sky last night, Grey Rabbit," he called. "That rocket went to the stars."

Grey Rabbit took the shining thing and pinned it to her apron.

"A present from out of the air," said she. "It's a lost spark from the bonfire, or it may be a shooting star."

"I think it's Guy Fawkes' tie-pin," Fuzzypeg said. "He sent it to us because he was too busy to come."

HARE'S RECIPE FOR BONFIRE TOFFEE

Take some butter, and a pawful of brown sugar. Put them in Grey Rabbit's saucepan. Add a bit of honeycomb, an eggcupful of spring water, and a pinch of lavender or rosemary leaf. Boil till a drop hardens when you let it fall in some water. Then hurry and pour it out on a buttered plate. Leave it to cool. Grey Rabbit will cut it into squares ready for Bonfire night.